D0190898

Please return / renew by date shown.
You can renew it at:
norlink.norfolk.gov.uk
or by telephone: 0344 800 8006
Please have your library card & PIN ready

Read Stack Oct 16

NORFOLK LIBRARY
AND INFORMATION SERVICE

Also by Anthony Horowitz from
Macmillan Children's Books

LEGENDS: BATTLES AND QUESTS

LEGENDS: BEASTS AND MONSTERS

LEGENDS: DEATH AND THE UNDERWORLD

LEGENDS: HEROES AND VILLAINS

LEGENDS: TRICKS AND TRANSFORMATIONS

LEGENDS

ANTHONY HOROWITZ

THE WRATH OF THE GODS

Illustrated by Thomas Yeates

MACMILLAN CHILDREN'S BOOKS

First published 2012 by Macmillan Children's Books
a division of Macmillan Publishers Limited
20 New Wharf Road, London N1 9RR
Basingstoke and Oxford
Associated companies throughout the world
www.panmacmillan.com

ISBN 978-0-330-51030-1

1 3 5 7 9 8 6 4 2

A CIP catalogue record for this book is available from
the British Library.

Printed and bound by CPI Group (UK) Ltd, Croydon CR0 4YY

CONTENTS

INTRODUCTION

Imagine you were born ten thousand years ago. You're sitting in your cave at night watching the sun set and you feel a sense of dread as the darkness, black and impenetrable, stretches out across the land. There are no electric lights, no TV, no books, nothing except a fire which you can light to keep yourself warm and which provides you with a sense of safety.

Where has the sun gone? You have absolutely no idea how the universe works, that the world is spinning and in orbit. You examine the bright lights in the sky and the fact that you are looking at a thermonuclear fusion of hydrogen – in other words, a star – escapes you. There's a storm, and a bolt of lightning suddenly comes crashing down. What has happened? Is there somebody 'up there' who has become angry? And as you settle down to sleep, an awful thought crosses your mind. How can you be sure that the sun will rise again in the morning and what on earth will you do if it doesn't?

I can't pretend I'm any great expert on this subject, and everything I'm writing in this introduction may be quite wrong, but I've always thought that this is how myths must have begun. People needed explanations for the world that was around them, and the most imaginative of them – the shamans or the storytellers – began to weave together stories that did just that.

The ancient Greeks were the most imaginative of all and, perhaps helped by the fact that their country was so beautiful and generally lacking in the extremes that inflicted other parts of the world – drought and famine, for example – they created some of the most poetical and enduring myths of all.

Take the sunrise. They looked at the mountains that soared above them and imagined a place called Olympus, where a family of gods lived. The father of the gods they called Zeus (the name may come from the Sanskrit word, *dyaus*, meaning day) and he had a son called Apollo who had a golden chariot that was pulled by fiery horses across the world. Apollo was, of course, the sun-god, and by praying to him and making sacrifices the Greeks ensured that he would continue to do his work and bring light to them every day.

And as the story was told and retold it became more elaborate – as all stories do. The storytellers saw the sunbeams slanting down, so they gave Apollo a bow and golden arrows. He became a shepherd god, a god of music and, perhaps because the truth will always come to light, a god of prophecy with a famous oracle on the island of Delphi.

Perhaps to make him more real they began to tell stories about his exploits. In one, for example, he was challenged to a musical contest by a satyr (a woodland spirit) called Marsyas, who was a great flute player. Apollo played a stringed instrument – a lyre – and won the contest when he challenged Marsyas both to sing and to play his flute at the same time which was, of course, impossible. Apollo won and, as a punishment, he tore the skin of Marsyas and nailed it to a tree . . . and the moral of this is that you should never challenge a god (see the ten rules at the back of this book).

There was another reason for the creation of myths, and that was to explain the way human beings behaved. If the gods did it, then it was OK for people to do it too. Look at the way Zeus went around chasing women . . . and boys for that matter. Or Dionysius with his drunken banquets. It was often quite convenient for a god to behave badly, because then kings and princes could do exactly the same themselves.

And these stories were so successful that they are with us to this very day. What was the name of the first rocket that went to the moon? The planets are named after gods – as are the days of the week. (Thursday, for example, finds its origin in Thor, whom you'll meet within these pages). How many constellations can you think of? Here are a few – Orion, Aries, Hercules, Pegasus, Cassiopeia. They're all named after figures in mythology. Heroes of mythology turn up in everything from chocolate bars to new automobiles.

One interesting question I sometimes wonder about is: Where do myths end and modern religions begin? Nobody believes in Zeus or

Apollo any more, but millions believe in a God (with a capital G) of one sort or another. Look at the Bible. Most people would agree that the Garden of Eden with its apple and its talking snake didn't really exist. Does that make it a myth? But what about the stories of the miracles of Christ? I think you'd be on very dangerous ground if you used the word 'myth' in that context.

Anyway, that's the end of this unusually serious introduction. In this collection you will find answers to all sorts of questions that taxed those ancient but very creative minds. How was mankind invented? How was the first fire made? Why are there so many bad things in the world? How did the terrible war of Troy begin? I'm not sure what the story of Senda is all about – but I hope you enjoy it anyway.

The Wrath of the Gods is quite a good title, I think. Whenever the gods got angry, the entire world changed, usually for the worse and I hope that if any of them happens to read this, they won't take offence.

Anthony Horowitz

PANDORA'S BOX

Greek

Pandora's Box

A long, long time ago there was a great battle between the gods and a race of giants who were known as Titans. From the very start, this was an unequal struggle.

The gods, of course, were incredibly powerful, quick-witted and skilled in the art of war. First there was Zeus, the king of Olympus, armed with lethal thunderbolts. Then there was Poseidon (the sea god) with his trident, Apollo (the sun god) with his golden arrows and Hermes (the messenger god) who could turn himself invisible. Together they were an invincible army as anyone with any sense would have been able to see.

Unfortunately the Titans – though very large and immensely strong – had the same problem that afflicts many of the giants who turn up in stories like this. They just weren't very bright. A Titan might tear up a mountain instead of going round it, but he would probably forget where he was going in the first place. A Titan might be able to hurl a

rock the size of Gibraltar a hundred miles or more, but he would always miss what he was aiming for. When two Titans met, they might shake hands or tear each other's arms off. It all depended on their mood.

By far the smartest of the Titans was a giant called Prometheus, and it is with him that this story begins. He realized pretty quickly that the battle couldn't be won and refused to take part. Sure enough the other Titans were defeated so quickly that the entire war was over by lunchtime and all of them were sent to a dark, rat-infested prison in the depths of Tartarus. Prometheus alone was spared. And to show just how much he admired the gods, he took a little clay and water and created a whole tribe of strange little creatures who looked just like them.

These creatures were the first men.

Prometheus loved his creations in the same way parents love their children. He was immensely proud of everything they did, boasted about them to almost anyone who would listen and generally fussed over them as if they could do no wrong. One thing he never gave them though was food. Instead, he fed them knowledge – scraps of information which he picked up from Athene (the goddess of wisdom), who happened to be his closest friend. One day she would tell him about mathematics and straight away he would rush down to earth to pass it on. The next day it might be art or architecture or even quantum physics. It's strange to think that our entire civilization could have been handed down to us rather in the manner of dog biscuits – but that was how it was.

As the years passed and mankind became more intelligent, Zeus, who had been watching all this from his celestial throne, grew uneasy.

'I'm a little worried about these human beings,' he remarked to his wife, the goddess Hera, as they shared a goblet of wine.

'What about them?' Hera asked.

'Well, I just wonder if they're not getting a bit . . . above themselves. Where will it all lead to? Today the basics of maths and science, tomorrow they could be flying to the moon!'

'I hardly think so,' Hera laughed. 'But what are you going to do about it?'

'I don't know. But I'm keeping my eye on them . . . !'

Zeus was a jealous god, but he wasn't cruel enough to destroy the newly formed human race, so mankind continued to flourish. But everything went wrong one day in a place called Sicyon. The trouble was all down to a question of sacrifice, and it was Prometheus who was entirely to blame.

There had been a feast at Sicyon and, as usual, a special sacrificial bull had been chosen to honour Zeus. But as he looked at the magnificent animal, Prometheus began to wonder why all the best bits were reserved for the gods. After all, it was man who had worked hard to raise the animal in the first place so why should he have to give it all away?

So, very unwisely, Prometheus decided to

play a trick on the gods. When the bull had been killed and cut up, he took two sacks. Into one of these he put all the most delicious cuts of meat – rump steak and fillet steak, the sirloin and the rub. But he concealed them underneath the stomach bag which was all white and rubbery and generally unpleasant to look at. Then he took a second sack and put all the most disgusting parts of the bull into it – the bones, the gristle, the eyeballs and the hoofs. But he covered these with a layer of fat to make them look as delicious as possible.

Finally, he took both the sacks and knelt before Zeus.

'O mighty king,' he said. 'I would like your opinion on the question of sacrifice. Nobody can decide which parts of the animal should go the gods and which parts should remain to be enjoyed by humans. Why don't you choose?'

It never occurred to Zeus that a Titan could be so devious and he was completely

deceived. He chose the bones and the fat, and ever since, the gods have been given nothing else from the sacrifice. However, when he found out how Prometheus had tricked him, he was furious.

'Very well!' he thundered. 'Mankind can have his steak. But he will eat it raw!'

And with those words he reached out with one hand and snatched all the fire from the world.

Mankind had got the worst deal after all. Without fire they could take no pleasure in their food, and once the sun had gone down they could only stay indoors, huddled under animal skins for warmth. But Prometheus was willing to do anything to help his creation, and one day, while Zeus was away, he stole up to Olympus. Athene was still his friend and she let him in through a side door. At once Prometheus strode up to the sun and, using his bare hands, he broke off a blazing fire-brand. This he carried back to earth, thrusting it into a giant fennel leaf.

And, in this way, people were once again about to come out at night and enjoy grilled meat beneath the stars.

But this time Prometheus had gone too far. When Zeus heard how he had been defied for a second time, his anger exploded.

'Prometheus!' he shouted. 'You cheated me once and I forgave you because of your loyalty to me in the war of the Titans. But this time you must pay for your crimes. I am going to make an example of you that the world will never forget.'

And, so saying, he seized Prometheus and chained him to a pillar on the freezing slopes of the Caucasian mountains. But this was only the start of it. Every morning a huge vulture landed on the wretched Titan's chest, and even as he screamed in rage and horror the huge bird tore out his liver and devoured it. And every night, while Prometheus shivered in the sub-zero temperatures, his liver grew whole again. In this way the horrible torture could be repeated again

and again until the end of time.

Zeus punished mankind too. But as man hadn't really done anything wrong, his punishment was slightly different.

First Zeus visited the crippled god Hephaestus who worked at a great forge in Olympus with twenty bellows pumping twenty-four hours a day. Although ugly and misshapen himself, Hephaestus was incredibly skilful, the greatest blacksmith of all time.

'I want you to make a woman,' the king of the gods commanded. 'I want her to be more beautiful than any woman ever seen on the face of the earth. She must be perfect. As perfect as a goddess.'

The crippled god did as he was told. He had only ever disobeyed Zeus once . . . that was how he had become crippled. Now he fashioned a woman out of clay, moulding her perfect features with his bare hands. He asked the four winds to breathe life into her and approached all the goddesses to dress her in their finest clothes and jewels.

The result was Pandora.

Zeus was delighted when he saw the blacksmith-god's work and instructed Hermes to carry her straight down to the world. As soon as she arrived she was married to King Epimetheus, who was actually the brother of Prometheus and the only other Titan who had not joined in the war against the gods.

Now Epimetheus had been warned never

to trust the gifts of Zeus. But seeing the terrible fate that had befallen his brother he was too afraid to refuse. And he had to admit that Pandora was very beautiful. You'd have had to be mad to think otherwise. When she walked into the room, men fell silent and all eyes turned on her. When she spoke, everyone listened. When she made jokes, they all laughed. In fact, whatever she did was greeted with applause, and Epimetheus had to admit that he did feel rather proud to be married to her.

Pandora's Box

Unfortunately the one thing that Pandora had not been given by the gods was a great brain. She never had anything interesting to say, and although Epimetheus did his best to be a kind and attentive husband, she made him a poor and unfaithful wife. This was all part of Zeus's revenge. He had made her as shallow and as empty-headed as she was beautiful. And she was going to cause mankind more trouble than any human being before or since.

For Epimetheus owned a large ebony box that was kept in a special room in his palace, guarded day and night. In this box he had collected and imprisoned all the things that could harm mankind. It was the one room

in the palace that Pandora was forbidden to enter, and naturally it was the one room that most aroused her curiosity.

'I bet you keep all sorts of interesting things in that big black box of yours,' she would say in her syrupy voice. 'Why don't you let your little Pandy look inside?'

'It is not for you, my dear,' Epimetheus would reply. 'You should leave it well alone.'

'But . . .'

'No, no, my love. Trust me. No one may open the box.'

'Then you don't love me,' Pandora would cry, crossing her arms and pouting. 'I wish I'd never met you. I hate it here!'

They had this conversation many times, until the day when Pandora's curiosity finally got the better of her. It would have been much better really if Epimetheus had told her what was inside the box. She was certain that it contained something special that he was holding back from her.

'I'll show him!' she muttered to herself.

'Why should he be allowed to keep anything from me?'

Waiting until Epimetheus was out, she managed to talk her way past the guards and slipped into his room. She had stolen the key from beside his bed and nobody thought to stop her. Was she not, after all, the king's wife and the mistress of the house? The box was right in front of her and, her whole body trembling, she knelt down and examined it. It was smaller and older than she had expected. She was also surprised – and a little alarmed – that the padlock which fastened it was in the shape of a human skull. But she was still certain it would contain treasure such as would make her own diamonds and pearls seem like mere pebbles. She turned the key and opened the box . . .

. . . and at once all the spites and problems that Epimetheus had kept locked up for so long exploded into the world. Old age, hard work, sickness . . . they flew out in a great cloud of buzzing, stinging, biting insects. It was as if Pandora had accidentally split the atom. One moment she was kneeling there with a foolish grin on her face. The next she was screaming in the heart of an intense darkness that had stripped her of her beauty and brought her out in a thousand boils.

At that moment, all the things that made life difficult today streamed out of Pandora's box and into the world.

Old age, hard work, sickness, vice, anger, envy, lust, jealousy, spite, sarcasm, cynicism, violence, intolerance, injustice, infidelity, famine, drought, plague, warfare, religious persecution, taxation, inflation, pollution, unemployment, fascism, fanaticism, racism, sexism, terrorism, communism, Blairism, nepotism, cubism, patriotism, nihilism, totalitarianism, plagiarism, vandalism, tourism, tabloid journalism, paranoia, kleptomania, claustrophobia, xenophobia, hypochondria, insomnia, megalomania, narrow-mindedness, thoughtlessness,

selfishness, bribery, corruption, censorship, gluttony, pornography, delinquency, vulgarity, illiteracy, dishonesty, bureaucracy, obesity, acne, diplomatic immunity, battery farming, traffic congestion, party political broadcasts, prefabricated concrete, fast food, muzak, TV talent contests, dolphinariums, organized crime, political correctness, health and safety, advertising, alcoholism, drug addiction, monosodium glutamate, nicotine, nuclear waste, drizzle, elephants' feet wastepaper baskets and much, much more.

At the last minute, Epimetheus rushed in and managed to slam down the lid, by which time only one thing was left in the box: hope.

Which is just as well. For with all the problems that Pandora had released into the world, where would we be without it?

THE JUDGEMENT OF PARIS

Greek

The intrigues of the gods of Ancient Greece often had far-reaching effects on the affairs of men. The divine inhabitants of Mount Olympus were completely unpredictable and what might begin the day as a happy occasion, a cause for celebration, could by sunset have become a bloodbath that would cast crimson shadows over the world for years to come. Just such an event was the marriage of Peleus and Thetis. For it was the first signpost on the road that would lead, through many twists and turns, to the ten terrible years of the Trojan War.

Peleus and Thetis

Thetis was one of the most beautiful of the Nereids, the immortal nymphs of the sea. She was so beautiful that Zeus, the king of the gods, had fallen in love with her. But she had coldly rejected him. Zeus was too old and unattractive and he was also married to Hera, who happened to be Thetis's foster mother. To get his revenge, Zeus had decreed that Thetis would never marry an immortal and so Hera went out and searched the world for the perfect human being. She found Peleus.

Peleus was a king: young, handsome and the owner of a magic sword that made him the victor of any battle he fought.

'He may not be immortal,' Hera said. 'But, my dear, he's about as close as you're going to get.'

Thetis, furious at the thought of having to marry a mere human being, took herself off to a secluded island, riding naked across the sea on the back of a dolphin. But when she got there she found Peleus waiting for her. At once he threw himself on her, kissing her passionately. Thetis turned herself into fire. Peleus hung on. She turned herself into water. Peleus wouldn't let go. She became a lion, a serpent – even an octopus. Still Peleus clung to her even though he was by now burned, drenched, clawed, bitten, covered

in ink and very tired. At last Thetis yielded to him and discovered that Hera had indeed been telling the truth.

Never was there a wedding like that of Peleus and Thetis. It was celebrated at midnight on the gentle slopes of Mount Pelion.

As the couple exchanged their vows, they were lit by a full moon, by a confetti of stars and by a ring of blazing lamps, swaying in the olive trees. After the heat of the day, the breeze was soft and cool. Gods walked side by side with mortals, breathing in the scented midnight air. Centaurs cantered in the long grass with laughing Nereids on their backs. The nine Muses came down from heaven to sing the nuptials. The beautiful Ganymede himself, cup-bearer to the gods, poured nectar from a silver jug. For a short time the world was still and Peleus and Thetis were in love.

There was one goddess who had not been invited to the wedding. Her name was Eris and

as she was the goddess of
strife and discord, nobody
had wanted her to come.
Now she appeared, her
long, grey hair sprawling
over her shrivelled face, her
eyes aflame. In one skeletal
hand she held a golden
apple. As the music died
down and the guests stared
at her, she lifted it up. For
a moment the moonlight
caught the gold and it
seemed to explode, white,
above her head. Then, with
a shrill laugh, she threw it
down on to the ground and
without a word turned back
the way she had come.

The apple hit the ground
and rolled down a slope
to rest at the feet of three
goddesses who had been

talking together, arm in arm, when Eris had arrived. The three were Athene, goddess of wisdom, Aphrodite, goddess of love, and Hera. It was Hera who broke the silence.

'A present from Eris!' she exclaimed. 'Why don't you pick it up, Peleus?'

Peleus leaned down. As his palm surrounded it, the chill of the metal seemed to travel up his arm, shuddering through his veins until it reached his very heart.

It was far heavier than he would have thought possible. In seconds his wrists and shoulders were aching. He would have gladly thrown it away from him. Although the apple was made of gold it was somehow ugly. He could almost feel it draining the life out of him.

'Is there an inscription?' Athene asked. 'Who is it for?'

Peleus turned the apple clumsily in his hands. 'Yes,' he said. He could not lie. 'There is an inscription.'

'What does it say?' Aphrodite demanded.

The Judgement of Paris

'It . . . it . . .' The words died in his throat. Despite the breeze, he was sweating. He looked again at the three simple words cut into the gold surface of the apple. Three words. 'To the fairest,' he read out.

'To the fairest,' Hera repeated.

'The fairest,' Aphrodite muttered, smiling.

'And to which one of us are you going to give it?' Athene asked.

'I . . . I don't know.'

There often comes a moment at a party when something goes wrong and you know that no matter what you say or how much more wine you drink, nothing is going to make it right. That moment had now come to the wedding of Peleus and Thetis. Although the three goddesses were still smiling, their arms were no longer linked and their eyes were firmly fixed on the apple. The guests had formed a wide circle around them. Nobody was talking. Then Zeus stepped forward.

'We will not decide who deserves the apple tonight,' he said. 'That decision can be made at another time.'

'By whom?' Athene demanded.

'If you decide, you'll just give it to your wife,' Aphrodite said.

'And why not?' Hera cried. 'It was probably meant for me anyway.'

'A man shall decide,' Zeus interrupted. 'Paris, son of Priam, will be the judge.'

He took the apple from Peleus. Peleus stepped back, rubbing his palm. He looked up and shivered. A cloud had passed across the face of the moon. Suddenly it was cold.

Paris

Paris was the son of Priam and Hecuba, the king and queen of Troy. A few weeks before he had been born, his mother had had a horrible

nightmare. She had dreamed that instead of
a baby, she had given birth to a blazing log.
The log had fallen to the ground in a shower
of sparks and from the crumbling wood had
emerged a flood of fiery
worms. She had awoken
screaming that Troy
was on fire and it
was days before
she was able to
sleep again. Priam
had consulted a
seer to find out
what the dream
meant and this was
what he was told.

   'The child that is
about to be born will
destroy our country. If
you do not want to see Troy in
ruins and the blood of your other children
coagulating in the mud then, mighty Priam,
you must kill him immediately!'

When he heard the prophecy, Priam determined to kill the child himself. But when, a few days later, his wife was delivered of a healthy, gurgling boy, he could not find the heart to do it. Instead he gave the task to a man called Agelaus, who was his chief shepherd. Although Agelaus wasn't particularly happy about the order, he dared not disobey and left the child on a barren slope on Mount Ida, thinking he would quickly starve to death. But returning there five days later, he was astonished to find him still alive, for the boy had been suckled by a she-bear. With a sigh, he drew his sword. The baby laughed at him and his heart melted. Carrying the boy home in a wallet, he sent a dog's tongue to Priam, telling him that it came from his dead baby. He brought the boy up as his own son, calling him Paris which is the Greek word for wallet.

Nobody ever really believed that Paris was the true son of Agelaus. He was far too strong and quick-witted to be the son of a mere shepherd. But it was as a shepherd that he had been brought up. And it was while he was guarding his adoptive father's sheep on the heights of Mount Gargarus that Hermes, the messenger of the gods, came to him, accompanied by Hera, Athene and Aphrodite.

'Paris!' the messenger god exclaimed as his winged sandals carried him gently through the air. 'I come from Zeus, lord of Olympus. He has chosen you from all the mortals in the world to make a judgement.' He reached into his satchel and produced the apple. 'You must give this to one of the three goddesses that you see before you. But it is up to you to decide which is the fairest. For it is to the fairest of the three that this prize must be awarded.'

Paris took the apple, gazing at the three goddesses who were by this time neither holding hands, smiling nor even looking at one another.

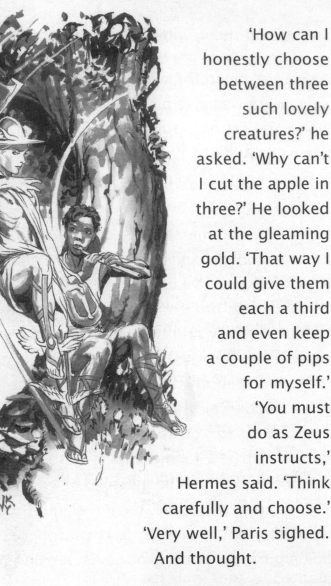

'How can I honestly choose between three such lovely creatures?' he asked. 'Why can't I cut the apple in three?' He looked at the gleaming gold. 'That way I could give them each a third and even keep a couple of pips for myself.'

'You must do as Zeus instructs,' Hermes said. 'Think carefully and choose.'

'Very well,' Paris sighed. And thought.

The Judgement of Paris

Hera

As well as being the wife of
Zeus, Hera was also his
sister. She sat on a golden
throne beside him on
Mount Olympus, doing
her best to ignore his
many love affairs. But she
was never unfaithful to
him herself.

She had appeared to
Paris as a young woman
wearing a long, simple
tunic with a crown of
leaves and blossoms
on her head and two
magnificent ear-rings, each
one made of three brilliant
diamonds, hanging from
her ears. Hera took great
care of her looks. Being
married to Zeus who ran

after just about every nymph, nereid and goddess that he saw (not to mention a fair number of young men too) she had no choice. Once a year she took herself off to swim in the magical waters of the spring of Canathus and when she returned, even Zeus would have to admit that she was lovelier than ever.

She was known as the goddess of the white arms, and as she walked in front of the young shepherd, he could not help but wonder at the purity of her skin. A peacock, her sacred animal, walked beside her, its tail open to exhibit an explosion of turquoise and emerald as if it thought that it could lend some of its own beauty to that of its mistress.

'Paris,' she said, stopping and throwing back her hair. 'I think you should think very, very carefully before you make up your mind. Far be it from me to influence your decision, but you might like to consider just how unwise it might be to have the wife of Zeus as your enemy. Poor Semele, for example . . . I had her burned to death. I turned Io into a cow which I suppose was appropriate. As for Hercules, well he'd gone right out of his mind by the time I'd finished with him.

'On the other hand,' and here she smiled sweetly, 'my generosity knows no bounds. How would you like to be the lord of all Asia, just for a start? Here you are working as a humble shepherd. I could make you the richest man in the world. Choose me, Paris. I am the fairest. The apple is rightfully mine.'

Athene

Athene was taller and thinner than Hera and wore neither jewellery nor ornament, carrying instead a sword and a shield. Until she had undressed, she had been wearing a rough cloak over a suit of armour with her head encased in a silver helmet. A face of unbelievable hideousness stared out of her shield which she now laid in the grass so as not to upset Paris. This was Medusa who had at one time been able to turn people into stone until, with Athene's help, she had been decapitated. The goddess of wisdom (and, on occasion, of war) was the daughter of Zeus and Metis, his first wife. She had been born in a very peculiar way. For Zeus, after an argument, had swallowed Metis whole. Everybody on Mount Olympus had been far too polite to mention this, and when Zeus went to bed with a blinding headache, they had all assumed it was guilt. In fact it was

The Judgement of Paris

Athene who leaped out of her father's head to his great astonishment but also, it must be said, to his relief.

Unlike virtually all the other gods and goddesses, Athene was completely chaste. When a young man, Tiresias, had accidentally spotted her swimming in the nude, she had immediately struck him blind. You can imagine, then, that she was hardly happy about parading herself in front of Paris and when she spoke she was short and sharp.

'Choose with wisdom, young man,' she said. 'So choose the goddess of wisdom. Choose me! . . . Gifts? What would the wife of Zeus know about gifts? Nothing! Who was it who gave mankind the first chariots, tamed the first horses, invented the pottery wheel and taught the art of weaving? Not old ivory-arms, I can tell you! Choose me and I will give you great wisdom. Choose me and you will never lose a battle.'

'I'm not sure I ever want to fight a battle,' Paris said. 'But thank you all the same.'

Aphrodite

The third goddess was no more beautiful than the other two but somehow Paris found himself most swiftly drawn to her. For Aphrodite was the goddess of love. The owner of a magic girdle that could instantly enslave god or man, she was the complete mistress of the art of seduction, a laughing, shameless, secretive immortal both envied and admired by her sisters on Mount Olympus.

And yet she was married to one of the most repulsive gods, the limping Hephaestus. Hera was the mother of Hephaestus and hence her mother-in-law. But she had no true parents of her own. She had been born on the foaming crest of a wave, carried across the sea by the West Wind and thrown, perfectly formed, on to the coast of Cyprus.

Now she stood naked before Paris and laughed at his discomfort.

'To the fairest,' she began. 'Already I think you have made up your mind, shepherd-boy.

The Judgement of Paris

I can see it by the blush in your young cheeks, the way you try to avoid my eyes. Well, Paris, if you are as wise as you are handsome, and you are very handsome, you will know what to do with this precious golden apple.

'You have been offered . . . this and that. Money, power, strength – mere bribes, and nothing to do with man's greatest pleasure. I think I can offer you something a little more . . . stimulating. How would you like to find yourself married to Helen?'

'Helen?' His mouth was dry.

'Yes. Helen of Sparta. I dare say you know her name.'

'Is she as beautiful as the stories say?' Paris asked.

'More beautiful.'

'But she is married . . .'

'That can be dealt with.'

'You promise?'

'I promise.'

'Then the apple is yours!'

Paris gestured and Hermes, who had been watching the contest in silence, stepped forward to give the prize to the winner. The apple seemed light in Aphrodite's hand and she held it as if she had never really wanted it in the first place. But Hera and Athene trembled with anger. While Aphrodite laughed, they gathered up their clothes and disappeared from Mount Gargarus to suffer their bitterness in solitude, consoling themselves with thoughts of revenge.

But all Paris could think of was the prize he had won by his judgement.

'Tell me about Helen,' he demanded. 'Many travellers have spoken of her. They say she is the most beautiful woman who ever lived. Is it true?'

'She is even more beautiful than I am,' Aphrodite said.

And with a smile that hid a dark and dangerous knowledge, she told him about the woman whose beauty was soon to cause the dreadful war of Troy.

Helen

'Among the many loves of Zeus there was a mortal woman, Leda by name, the wife of a certain King Tyndareus. Love? Zeus could have become the god of love himself, so healthy an interest did he take in its pleasures. Well, he knew that Leda was not for him. She was devoted to her husband for a start. And she would hardly let herself be seduced by a man old enough to be her father!

'And so he tricked her. One day, as she sat beside the River Eurotas, a white swan appeared, gliding silently towards her. How happy she was to see it, its feathers radiant in the sunlight! How she laughed as the swan brushed her bare legs with its wings. But the swan (of course you have guessed) was Zeus in disguise and while Leda was off her guard, he suddenly pounced. She struggled, but it was too late. From this brief encounter a child was born, a daughter whom she called Helen.

'How can I describe how lovely that young girl was, how talented, how charming? Suffice it to say that when she was barely ten years old, she was carried off by none other than Theseus himself. The slayer of the Minotaur would gladly have made her his wife had not her two half-brothers arrived in the nick of time to carry her home. By the time she had reached the marrying age, her father's palace was filled to the brim with some of the finest young men in Greece, all of them as neatly pierced with Cupid's arrows as you could wish. Who was there? Well, Ajax was one of them. Today he is one of the most admired warriors in the country. Then there was Patroclus, the cousin of Achilles, and . . . well, Helen was always surrounded by men and there were so many of them you never knew who exactly was there.

'In fact, her father, Tyndareus, became quite worried by the situation. He was afraid that once he announced the name of the lucky man, he would have a riot on his hands. And so it might have been, had he not forced all of them to swear a sacred oath that no matter who was chosen as Helen's husband, they would always come to his aid when he was in need. They swore, and when Prince Menelaus was named (he now rules as King of Sparta) they could do nothing but congratulate him, albeit rather grudgingly.

'They have been married now for three years, and very happily by all accounts. Why then, you may be wondering, should Helen want to leave him and run away with you? The answer to that, my dear Paris, is simple. When Tyndareus married Leda – this was long before her encounter with Zeus – he naturally made sacrifices to all the gods, as is the custom. Unfortunately, the foolish man left out one of the more important goddesses who swore that his children would be notorious for their adulteries. So you see, the marriage of Helen was doomed from the start. She was born an adulteress, and an adulteress she shall be.'

This was what Aphrodite told the shepherd. What she did not tell him was that it was she who had been forgotten at the wedding of Tyndareus. And by arranging

Helen's flight with Paris, she was not only paying the price for the golden apple. She was repaying a slight and fulfilling an ancient curse.

Troy

This has been a long and complicated story, a road with many twists and turns. Longer still was to be its conclusion, but we can move rapidly ahead.

Shortly after the judgement, Paris decided to attend the annual games held in the city of Troy. Here he was recognized by his father, King Priam, and welcomed back into the palace. No longer a shepherd but a prince, he sailed to Sparta where he cynically took advantage of the king's hospitality to steal away with his wife. Although the jealous Hera sent a storm to try to stop them, Paris and Helen sailed safely back to Troy. The Trojan people fell in love with the Greek queen the moment they saw her. Soon she was delivered of three sons: Bunomus, Aganis and Idaeus. For a time, they were happy.

But Paris had been deceived by Aphrodite and had underestimated the wrath of Menelaus. The King of Sparta was enraged not only by the theft of his wife but by the underhand method in which it had been accomplished – while Paris was a guest in his own house. Helped by his brother Agamemnon, he set about raising an army the size of which had never been seen nor even dreamed of before. He began with all the kings and princes who had once been the suitors of Helen, the same men who had sworn to come to his aid. To these he added just about every great warrior alive: Odysseus, Achilles (the son of Peleus and Thetis), Nestor, Diomedes ... and many more.

They came to Aulis, a secluded beach in the Euboean straits. Soon there were so many men lining the shore that you could no longer see the sand. The fleet, stretching as far as the horizon, was like an incredible floating city. After sacrificing to Zeus and Apollo, the fleet departed, slowly sailing into a sun that was as cruel as the sacrificial flames.

They would not return until the great city of Troy was utterly destroyed, its sons killed and maimed, its daughters sold as slaves. This was the legacy that Paris brought his countrymen. This was the fate that his mother had once foretold.

Virtually all the men and women who have played a part in this story were to die. Not one single person would escape his share of suffering. And seventeen years would pass before Menelaus and Helen were reunited.

The marriage of Peleus would soon collapse. All his children would die, Achilles falling with a poisoned arrow in his heel. King Priam too would see the corpses of many of his children before he was himself slaughtered on the altar of his palace. Captivity in Greece awaited Queen Hecuba. She would finally be transformed into a dog, baying at the moon in her madness and grief. Ajax, Patroclus, Agamemnon, the three sons of Paris . . . and Paris himself. They would all die.

And what of the gods and goddesses with whom the story began? Although they would watch over the battlefield, over the growing pools of blood; although they would sometimes help one side, sometimes the other, they would not die. For they were immortal. They would not even suffer.

As flies to wanton boys are we to the gods;
They kill us for their sport.
> (William Shakespeare, *King Lear*)

THE STOLEN HAMMER OF THOR

Norse

The Stolen Hammer of Thor

What we call Thursday was originally called Thor's day, for it was dedicated by the Vikings to Thor, the god of thunder and son of Odin who was himself king of the gods. Tall and strong, with a flowing red beard, Thor lived with his father in the citadel of Asgard which could only be reached by crossing a rainbow bridge. It was said by the Vikings that the sound of thunder was nothing more than the wheels of Thor's chariot rumbling over the clouds.

Thor possessed a pair of iron gloves and a magic belt that doubled his strength. His voice was so loud that it could be heard even above the clamour of a battle and would have his enemies fainting with terror. But his most prized possession was his hammer – Mjolnir – the Destroyer. Mjolnir had been made from a meteorite that had fallen to the earth during a storm. It had been fashioned into shape by a dwarf whose skill in ironwork was unrivalled. Using his strength, Thor could hurl the hammer at a target on the other side of the world. Never did it miss its mark. Once thrown, it always returned to his hand. Every year, Thor used Mjolnir to break up the ice of winter in order to allow spring to come once again.

You can imagine, then, how Thor felt when he woke up one day to find that his precious hammer was missing. He looked under his pillow, then under his bed. He tore the pillow to shreds, then the bed to matchwood. Finally, he ransacked every room in the house, knocking down several walls with his bare fists – but all to no avail.

It was then that Loki, the god of firelight, happened to pass. Seeing Thor sitting in the street with half the contents of the house and, indeed, half the house itself scattered around him, he asked what was the matter. Now Loki was a sly, untrustworthy god who delighted in mischief. Normally Thor wouldn't have trusted him as far as he could throw him (which was actually a very long way indeed) but by now he was so desperate, he told him everything.

'Don't worry, my dear fellow,' Loki said. 'I'll find Mjolnir for you. I expect one of the giants has stolen it.'

'The giants!' Thor's face lit up. 'Why didn't I think of that?'

'I can't imagine.' Loki smiled to himself, for he did not think very highly of Thor's intelligence. 'You wait here. I'll see what I can do.'

With that, Loki turned himself into a bird and flew out of Asgard, over the rainbow bridge and on to the frozen land of Jotunheim where the giants lived. Loki was sure he would find the hammer there, for the giants had never liked the gods and they actively hated Thor who had killed many of their number. But he was unsuccessful. Three times he flew around Jotunheim and he spied nothing. At last he settled beside a lake where, despite the ice that floated on

the surface, one of the giants was swimming.

'Having a good swim, your majesty?' he asked, for the giant was none other than Thrym, King of Jotunheim.

'Not cold enough,' Thrym replied, although his skin was quite blue and his beard had frozen solid. 'What brings you to Jotunheim, Loki?'

'A hammer,' Loki replied. 'Thor's hammer, to be precise.'

At that, Thrym roared with laughter. 'So he sent you, did he? Well, let me tell you something, my friend. You'll never find it!'

'So you know where it is?' Loki said.

'Of course I do. I was the one who stole it! And now I've hidden it eight fathoms underground, and only I know where.'

Once again the giant burst into laughter, icy drops of water splashing out of his hair.

Loki smiled politely. 'I imagine,' he began, 'that your majesty has some exchange in mind? The hammer is useless to you. What do you want for it?'

The giant stopped laughing. 'You are cunning, Loki,' he said, 'and you are right. For a long time now, I have been looking for a wife. Recently I heard talk of a certain Freya, the goddess

of love. I am told that she is very beautiful.'

'There is none more beautiful,' Loki agreed.

'Then I want her. The hammer will be my wedding present to her.'

'With respect,' Loki said, 'I'm not sure that Freya will be too happy about marrying you. I mean no offence, but your majesty is not exactly blessed with good looks. Your majesty's nose is crooked and the boil on your majesty's chin is the size of a steam pudding. Your majesty's stomach is also—'

'That's enough!' Thrym roared. 'If I don't get Freya, Thor doesn't get the hammer. And that's final!'

Loki returned to Asgard and found Thor, still sitting outside the wreckage of his house. Thor stood up hopefully, but his face fell when he saw that Loki had come back empty-handed. Then Loki told him what he had found out and once again he cheered up.

'That's simple, then,' he cried. 'We'll tell Freya and, in no time at all, I'll have my beloved Mjolnir back.'

'My dear Thor,' Loki sighed. 'Do you really think Freya will agree to marry Thrym? He's a giant, for goodness sake! And anyway, Freya is already married.'

'Oh yes,' Thor said. 'I hadn't thought of that. But let's ask her anyway, Loki. You never know.'

'No . . .' Loki agreed.

'Never!' Freya cried.

Thor and Loki stood sheepishly while

the goddess of love
glared at them with
remarkably little
love in her eyes.

'Never!' she
repeated. 'Thrym
is a disgusting
old giant. He has
a boil on his chin
the size of a
steam pudding.
I'm sorry, Thor,
but I wouldn't
marry him if
he was the last
creature alive.
It's preposterous
even to think of
it.'

'But my
hammer . . .' Thor muttered.

'Forget it!' Freya cried and slammed the
door.

Thor looked sadly at Loki, who shrugged. 'We'd better call a meeting of the council,' he said. 'This needs talking about.'

And so all the gods and goddesses of Asgard (apart from Freya and her husband) assembled in Odin's palace to decide what should be done, while Thor sat waiting for someone to come up with a good idea. He listened while they debated, shaking his head when one of the gods suggested he should enter Jotunheim alone to confront the king.

'It's impossible,' he said. 'I am virtually powerless without my hammer. Perhaps I could defeat Thrym, but not his entire court . . .'

'I could come with you,' another god suggested.

'No.' Again Thor shook his head. 'I cannot risk the life of my friends in such a venture. And anyway, what good would it do? If we killed Thrym, we'd never find out where Mjolnir was buried.'

The Stolen Hammer of Thor

At last Loki got to his feet and stepped into the centre of the crowded council chamber. As all eyes turned on him, he couldn't stop a mischievous smile flickering across his lips.

'I have an idea,' he said.

'What is it, Loki?' Odin demanded.

'It's simple really,' Loki explained. 'Thrym wants Freya. Freya won't go. But suppose Thor were to go to Jotunheim disguised as Freya . . . ?'

He got no further. With a great roar, Thor sprang forward.

'Are you saying I should dress up as a woman?' he demanded.

'Exactly,' Loki replied. 'You'll have to shave your beard off, of course. And your legs. But it seems to me to be the only way.'

'Why can't you go?'

'Because when Thrym gave me the hammer, I wouldn't know what to do with it. None of us would. It's your hammer. You'll have to go.'

'Dressed as a woman?' Thor pounded his fist into his palm. 'Thor, the god of thunder, wearing women's clothes? Never, Loki! I would die of shame!'

'You do Loki wrong, my son.' Now Odin got to his feet. 'It is a good idea. A cunning idea. There is no shame in it.'

'The giants will laugh at me, Father.'

'The giants will hardly be able to laugh when you have caved in their skulls,' Odin said.

'I won't go!'

'You will go! Mjolnir is not just a plaything. It is a great weapon and all Asgard relies on its strength. What will happen next spring if you cannot break the ice of winter? For it is a task you cannot do without Mjolnir. No, Thor. You will go. I, Odin, command it.'

There was a long silence. Then Thor nodded.

'Very well, Father,' he said. 'But if anyone laughs at me, I swear—'

'Nobody will laugh at you,' Odin promised.

But of course Loki was delighted by the whole affair. In fact the plan had been at the back of his mind from the very start which was why he had been so pleased to help. He never actually laughed at Thor, but he teased him unmercifully, simpering at him and calling him Thora. He even offered to travel to Jotunheim with him so as to enjoy the joke to its end.

After the council meeting, Thor's hair was cut short and covered by a blond wig.

His beard was shaved off and his eyebrows were plucked. His legs were shaved and he was given a white silk dress. A smear of lipstick, a little eye shadow and a garland of flowers completed the transformation. Then he and Loki sneaked out of a back door, Loki shaking with silent mirth, and the two of them set off for Jotunheim.

Thrym was ecstatic when he saw the two figures appear. At once he prepared a great banquet in the hall of his castle with a fire roaring in the hearth and the best gold plate laid out on the tables. He even put a plaster over the boil on his chin so that it would not offend his new bride. It did, perhaps, surprise him that Freya was well over six feet tall. As he took her arm to help her out of the chariot, he was a little puzzled by the bulging muscles beneath the silk dress. The way she walked, with great, manly strides, did seem a touch out of character. But Thrym was too excited to realize that he was being deceived.

As the evening wore on, however, it was impossible not to notice that something strange was going on. When the banquet was served, for example, Freya ate a whole ox, eight large salmon, fifteen loaves of bread, six plates of sweetmeats and well over thirty cakes, and drank three barrels of mead before half the guests had even picked up their knives and forks. Thrym stared at Thor, then Loki, then Thor again and rubbed his eyes.

'Forgive my asking, my dear,' he said. 'But is this the way the goddesses of Asgard normally behave? Even giant women can't eat as much as I have just seen you consume. Do you always eat as much as that?'

'Er . . . um . . .' Thor muttered.

'The lady Freya has been fasting for eight days,' Loki interrupted hastily. 'She wanted to look her best for you, so . . .. so she went on a diet! She hasn't touched anything for eight days.'

'How kind of her!' Thrym exclaimed. 'And

now, I think, to show my appreciation, I will give her a little kiss.' And he leaned forward, his great lips oozing in the direction of Thor's cheek.

Thor, of course, was horrified. He sprang up, lightning flashing from his eyes.

'Why do your eyes flash so, my dear?' Thrym asked. 'What ever can be the matter with you?'

'Freya is tired.' Once again Loki had to come up with a fast answer, for there were at least two dozen giants in the banqueting hall and had the deception been discovered, the two of them would have been torn apart before they could say 'Smörgåsbord'. Smiling, Loki led Thor back to his seat. 'She hasn't been asleep for a week,' he continued. 'You see, she's been so excited about coming here. Her eyes are a little red. Nothing to worry about, though!'

The answer satisfied Thrym and he gave orders for his wedding present to Freya to be brought in and laid on her knees, as was the custom. The doors opened and two servants came in, carrying Mjolnir on a silver tray. The moment Thor held it, the need for pretence was over. Standing up, he threw off the wig and with one swing of his arm, cracked open Thrym's skull. As Odin had predicted, none of the giants laughed at him. They were too busy fleeing for their lives – but without success. Every time Mjolnir flew a giant fell until soon there were none left standing.

Thor and Loki returned to Asgard in their chariot at once. As they rode over the rainbow bridge, Thor turned to the god of the fireplace and laid a hand on his shoulder.

'This has been a strange adventure,' he said, 'and not one that I shall remember with much joy. Thor disguised as a woman! But I am sure I can rely on you, my good friend, never to remind me of it nor to tease me about it.'

'Of course you can rely on me, my dear Thora . . . I mean, my dear Thor,' Loki replied.

THE TEN FINGERS OF SEDNA

Inuit

The Ten Fingers of Sedna

The gods and goddesses of the Eskimos are more to be feared than admired, for, like the wind that howls across the Bering Straits and the snow that slices down on Hudson Bay, they are savage and without pity. The most feared of all of them is Sedna. Sedna the sea-goddess. Sedna the giant. Sedna with her bedraggled hair and gaping socket where one eye has been torn out.

Once Sedna was a beautiful young Eskimo girl, the only daughter of a widowed father. So beautiful was she that as she grew up, a great many young men came from near and far in the hope of marrying her. But Sedna was a vain, haughty girl, too well-aware of her own good looks. She enjoyed teasing the young men, leading them on one minute, rejecting them the next. Sometimes she would whisper tales or choose a favourite, just for the pleasure of seeing them fight over her. And they did fight. Men killed for love of Sedna, but she still refused to marry.

Then one day a man arrived at the village, a man much handsomer than any that had come before. The kayak he came in was decorated with jewels and more jewels glittered in the necklace that hung across his breast. He wore the finest furs and carried a spear of pure white ivory. The young man didn't even get out of his canoe. Instead, he called out to Sedna.

'Come with me, Sedna! Come and be my wife!'

'Why?' Sedna called back. 'What can you give me?'

'You shall live in my house on the edge of a cliff,' the young man cried. 'You will never be hungry for I will bring you meat every day. You will sleep on a bearskin with a blanket of feathers and you will never have to work.'

To Sedna, this sounded almost too good to be true. And the young man was very handsome. Without another thought, she packed her bags and got into the kayak, never to be seen by the villagers again.

The boat sailed away. For two days and two nights they sailed and the further they went, the more the young man seemed to change. First his ivory spear and jewels disappeared. Then his skins fell away to reveal a sort of undershirt of feathers. His eyes grew beady and the feathers spread across his face. But it was only when they arrived at his home that the spell was finally broken. For the man was not a man at all but a bird-spirit with the power to take on human form. Flying above the village he had seen Sedna and had determined to make her his wife – even if he had to use magic and trickery to do it.

The Ten Fingers of Sedna

So Sedna began life married to a bird. The house on the edge of the cliff turned out to be a nest perched on a rocky crag. The meat that the bird had promised her was nothing more than freshly killed gulls and kittiwakes. The blanket of feathers was the bird's own wing and although it was true that she never had to work, nor was she able to do anything except groan and cry and bitterly curse the day that she had left the village.

The story might have ended there had her father not grown more and more lonely without her. She had never been a perfect daughter, it was true, but when you have only one daughter and your wife is dead, you are ready to overlook temper tantrums and whining and general ungratefulness. So he set out to search for her and after a great many weeks he found her still sitting in the nest bemoaning her fate.

By a stroke of luck, the bird-spirit was away, searching for food for his wife (she had demanded something a bit more delicate than freshly killed kittiwake) so she was able to tell her father what had happened.

'He's not a man, he's a bird!' she wailed. 'And I want to go home!'

'My poor child—' the father began.

'Don't you "poor child" me!' Sedna cried. 'If you'd only looked after me a little better this would never have happened. Now let's get moving. He'll be back any minute.'

The father helped his daughter climb down the cliff. They reached the bottom and ran across the beach to where his kayak was anchored. Sedna didn't want to get her feet wet and her father had to lift her into the boat and that wasted a bit of time, but soon they were sailing away, leaving the nest far behind them.

But then the bird-spirit returned. It saw the empty nest, the footprints in the sand and the boat, already just a speck on the horizon, and let out a great cry. For in its own way it had loved Sedna. It alone had been blind to her faults and it really had tried to make her happy in the nest.

Now it soared after them, its great white wings carrying it swiftly across the sea. In minutes it had reached the boat, hovering in the air above it, its eyes filled with tears.

'Come back, Sedna!' it cried. 'You are my wife. I need you!'

'Go away!' Sedna replied. 'Do you really think I'm going to spend my life married to a bird? Leave me alone!'

'Please . . .'

The bird-spirit swooped down as if to perch on the edge of the boat and at that moment the father swung his oar. The wood crashed into the bird-spirit, knocking it over backwards. The poor creature almost plunged into the sea, but then it recovered and, realizing that it had lost Sedna forever, flew away, crying softly.

The Ten Fingers of Sedna

The bird-spirit had no sooner disappeared than the weather changed. The surface of the sea had been still and flat but now an Arctic storm sprang up. The waves rose and fell. Icy cold water pounded against the boat, spinning it out of control. The father struggled with the oars but it was useless. The spray blinded him. The wind tore at his clothes. Black clouds had smothered the sky and now forks of lightning crackled down all around them.

'Do something!' Sedna cried. 'Don't just sit there . . . !'

'It's your fault!' her father exclaimed in a hoarse voice. 'The sea is angry because you've left your husband.'

There was a deafening crash of thunder. A wave as high as a mountain rose up beside them, almost turning the boat upside down.

'We're going to die!' Sedna wept. 'Why didn't you just leave me where I was? If you hadn't come for me, this would never have happened. If you . . .'

But then she stopped because a mad look had come into her father's eyes. Somehow he stood up in the rocking boat and grabbed hold of her.

'What are you doing?' she demanded.

'It's your fault,' her father rasped. 'And perhaps if I throw you overboard . . . yes . . . if I throw you overboard, then the sea will forgive me, then everything will be all right.'

'You're mad! Leave me alone!'

'You must die, Sedna. I should never have come for you.'

As the boat heaved up and down and whirled round in circles, as the lightning flashed and the thunder roared, the two of them fought in the tiny boat. At one point it seemed that Sedna might win, for she was the taller and the stronger of the two, but then somehow her father's thumb found her eye. There was another crash of thunder. Blood poured down her cheek. She staggered backwards and fell overboard.

But still she clung on to the edge of the

boat, desperately trying to pull herself back in. With an insane laugh, the father seized his ivory axe. With the wind racing around him, he held it high above his head, then brought it hurtling down. It severed five of Sedna's fingers.

Sedna screamed.

The fingers fell into the foaming sea and turned into seals.

The father struck again with the axe.

Sedna screamed a second time.

The five fingers of her other hand fell into the water and became whales. Sedna disappeared beneath the surface.

The storm died down and the sea grew calm. Unable to go any further, the father turned the boat in towards the shore and pitched his tent on a rocky outcrop on the edge of the beach. He knew that he had done wrong but he was too exhausted and too glad to be alive. Almost at once he fell into a deep sleep.

That night there was an unusually high

tide. The water came in further than it had ever done before, further than it has ever done since. It came in so far, in fact, that the old man drowned in his sleep. And as the waves lapped over one another, you could almost imagine that the sound they made was the sound of laughter.

NARcISSUS

Greek

Narcissus

Narcissus was the most beautiful young man in all of Ancient Greece – at least, in the opinion of Narcissus. The blind prophet Tiresias had once foretold that he would live to a ripe old age, provided that he never knew himself. Unfortunately, Narcissus knew himself all too well.

Every morning when he woke up, the first thing he would do would be to examine himself in his full-length mirror. He would run a hand through his long, blond hair. He would wink with one of his bright blue eyes. He would flex his muscles and smile at himself with perfect, white teeth. Then he would slip on a chiton (a short tunic) and go down to breakfast.

His parents had no idea what to do with him for although he was only sixteen years old, he was in truth remarkably good-looking. Half the girls in the country seemed to have fallen in love with him and the trouble was, he was so impossibly vain that he broke hearts left, right and centre.

One girl, for example, had sworn that she would kill herself if Narcissus wasn't a little kinder to her. His only response had been to send her a sword! The wretched girl had run herself through with it and that had been the end of her.

But it wasn't only humans who were bowled over by Narcissus. Greece was also filled with nymphs, charming spirits who peopled the rivers and springs, haunted the glades and mountains and guarded the trees in the forests. One of these was called Echo, and falling in love with Narcissus was the second bad

98

thing that happened in her life.

The first had been to play a trick on Hera who, as wife of Zeus and queen of the gods, was not known for her forgiving nature. Echo had distracted her by singing while Zeus slipped away to enjoy himself with another nymph he had happened to meet and when Hera had found out she'd been furious. She had punished Echo by forbidding her the power of speech, and at the same time condemning her always to repeat the last words anybody spoke to her.

So when Echo tried to tell Narcissus what she felt about him, she was only able to use his words. The result was disastrous.

She met him one day in a forest. Narcissus had supposedly gone out to hunt stags, but it was really too hot for hunting and besides he was afraid he would muss up his hair or ruffle his clothes. He was wandering down a leafy path when he saw the nymph gazing nervously at him. He yawned.

'Hello,' he muttered. 'I suppose you're yet

another of these women who find me so very attractive.'

'So very attractive,' Echo replied.

'I thought so,' Narcissus said. 'Well, you're wasting your time, I'm afraid.'

'I'm afraid,' Echo said.

'And so you ought to be,' Narcissus continued. 'To be absolutely honest, even if you were Aphrodite herself, I wouldn't let you come near me.'

'Come near me!' Echo cried.

'Are you deaf or something? I just told you I wouldn't. Now go away!'

'Away!' Echo moaned.

Realizing that her plight was hopeless, the nymph fled from the wood, tears pouring down her cheeks. She spent the rest of her short life heartbroken and alone in a desolate valley, living in a cave. Her flesh disappeared. Her bones turned to stone. Soon all that was left of her was her voice – and should you ever find yourself in a valley or a cave and call out, you will still hear her reply.

Meanwhile, Narcissus continued on his way, wondering what he should wear for supper that night and whether his hair would look even better if he parted it on the left. But it so happened that Aphrodite had heard his last remark to Echo and had seen what had taken place. And she was angry. For Aphrodite was the goddess of love and Narcissus had, by his words and deeds, made himself love's enemy. She put a curse on him by making him fall in love with himself.

Narcissus had always loved himself more than was proper, but once he had fallen under the spell of Aphrodite, he was lost. On his way home, he came upon a pool of crystal water in a clearing in the forest. It was a hot, sunny day and he knelt down to take a drink. That was when he saw what was – in his eyes – the most beautiful boy in the world. His mouth fell open. So did the boy's. His eyes blinked with astonishment. So did the boy's. He smiled. The boy smiled back. He had fallen in love with his own reflection.

The next day, his parents – who had been searching everywhere for him – found him still sitting beside the pool.

'Narcissus!' they exclaimed. 'What are you doing? We've been so worried about you.'

'Hush!' Narcissus whispered. A single tear trickled out of the corner of his eye. 'You'll frighten him away.'

'Frighten who away?' his mother asked.

'The boy,' Narcissus replied. 'He is so

beautiful . . . and yet so cruel. For when I reach out to touch him or try to kiss him he runs away from me.' He reached out and touched the surface of the water and sure enough, the reflection shimmered and disappeared. 'But he comes back after a while,' Narcissus continued, his voice soft and far-away. 'See! There he is now. Hasn't he got lovely eyes?'

'The boy's gone mad!' his father muttered.

'Come into the house, Narcissus dear,' his mother said. 'You haven't had supper or breakfast and you'll catch your death of cold sitting out here all night.'

'No! No!' Narcissus cried. 'I can't leave him. Not ever!'

And despite everything his parents said, he refused to move. All day and all night he lay in the long grass, his head propped up in his hands, gazing silently at his reflection. They brought him food. He wouldn't touch it. His torment was all the worse because although the object of his love was only a few inches away, they could never touch, they could never meet.

At last the pain became too much for him. It seemed to him that the boy in the pool had suffered too, for his face was terribly thin and his eyes were red and sore.

'I have hurt you at least as much as you have hurt me,' Narcissus whispered. His hand reached for the dagger that he wore in his belt. 'I shall hurt you no more.'

He plunged the knife into his heart. He screamed. The boy screamed. And somewhere, far away, Echo cried out too.

Narcissus died. And Aphrodite, taking pity on him, turned his body into a flower as a reminder of what had happened. And to this day, narcissus flowers can be found, growing wild in the woods and sprouting round the banks of a silent pool.

HOW TO SURVIVE THE GREEK GODS

A GUIDE FOR EVERY MORTAL

The Greek gods frequently involve themselves with the affairs of mankind – and unfortunately it doesn't always end happily. If you are on holiday in Greece and are approached by one of the gods, the following rules may help you. Do remember however that gods are, by their very nature, unpredictable, and if you find yourself slain, torn apart or turned into a snail, the author and the publisher of this book cannot be held responsible.

1. NEVER FALL IN LOVE WITH A GOD OR A GODDESS

It nearly always ends unhappily. The case of King Ixion comes to mind. He fell in love with Hera and as a result ended up tied to a burning wheel of fire. If you meet a naiad – run! These are river gods and goddesses who have a bad habit. When they fall in love with you . . . they drown you.

2. NEVER BE LOVED BY A GOD OR A GODDESS

Callisto was a nymph who was loved by Zeus. As a result she was turned into a bear. Io was a priestess and another of Zeus's lovers. She ended up as a cow and, worse still, was chased across the world by stinging flies.

3. YOU CAN'T SAY NO

Well you can, but it won't do you any good. When Zeus wanted to seduce Leda, he disguised himself as a swan. To reach Princess Danae, he fell on her as a torrent of golden coins. Syrinx was chased by the god Pan and tried to hide by turning herself into a bunch of reeds. He still cut her down and made her into a musical instrument. There's no escape!

4. BE CAREFUL WHERE YOU GO

Medusa was an attractive princess until she fell in love with the sea-god Poseidon. But the real mistake the two of them made was to sleep together in the temple of the goddess of wisdom, Athene. To punish her, Athene turned Medusa into a gorgon with hair made of living snakes.

5. BE CAREFUL WHERE YOU LOOK

Actaeon was a famous hunter who happened to spot the goddess Athene bathing naked. He was instantly turned into a stag and torn apart by his own hounds. This is not, I think, what is meant by a stag night.

6. DO NOT BETRAY THE GODS

The best example I can think of is King Sisyphus, who told someone where they could find one of Zeus's daughters . . . a small enough crime, you might think. He was sent straight to Hell, where he spent the rest of eternity rolling a huge boulder up a hill.

7. NEVER TRY TO TRICK THE GODS

You may have already read the story of Prometheus in this book. You might also consider King Tantalus, who invited the gods to a cannibal feast. He was sentenced to perpetual starvation in Hades, with delicious fruit and ice-cold water always inches from his lips.

8. WHATEVER THE GODS WANT, THE GODS GET

King Minos foolishly sacrificed his second best bull to the sea-god Poseidon. As a result, his wife gave birth to the half-man, half-bull monster known as the Minotaur.

9. BE MODEST

Captivated by his own beauty, Narcissus fell in love with himself, and look what happened to him. He wasted away. Famously, Arachne boasted that she was better at weaving than the goddess Athene. For this foolishness, the wretched girl was turned into a spider.

10. STAY AWAY FROM THE GODS

This is the best advice of all, really. Look at Paris, a humble shepherd who got drawn into a competition and ended up starting a long and terrible war. The truth is that the gods are always trouble, and even if one tries to help you you'll only end up making an enemy of another, just like Paris. So if you see one coming . . . run!

LEGENDS
BATTLES AND QUESTS

Brother fighting brother. Man slaying beast.
Tales of epic **quests** and furious **battles**
have been told throughout time –
Theseus and the **Minotaur**; **King Arthur**
and the **Black Knight**; Romulus and Remus,
and the **screams** of the Great Bell of Peking.
But there are some evils that no sword
can defeat . . .

**Rediscover classic myths and legends in these
action-packed retellings from Anthony Horowitz**

LEGENDS

BEASTS AND MONSTERS

In the cold, dead eyes of the **banshee** and the
hissing, spitting fangs of the **gorgon**; in the
fiery breath of the **dragon** and the razor-sharp
claws of the **sphinx** – there is a thirst for blood
and a **murderous** hunger.

But it is a time of heroes, and the teeth and
claws of these hideous beasts are no match for
the lethal blades of such men . . .

**Rediscover classic myths and legends in these
action-packed retellings from Anthony Horowitz**

LEGENDS

DEATH, AND THE UNDERWORLD

When life is **over**, and the conflicted souls of the **dead** wend their weary way down to the **underworld**, what do they see? A three-headed dog with **slavering jaws**, a dark and foreboding river with a skeletal ferryman, or simply **darkness**? Only the very brave or very foolish will venture down into the realm of the **afterlife** by choice, and they seldom live to tell the tale . . .

Rediscover classic myths and legends in these action-packed retellings from Anthony Horowitz

LEGENDS

HEROES AND VILLAINS

The battle between **good** and **evil** has raged throughout time.

The **heroes and villains** of this ancient conflict are many. Some fight using their superior **strength** and some their wit and cunning. Others triumph through **speed**, skill or sheer determination, but they all have one thing in common: they are ready to **fight to the death**.

Rediscover classic myths and legends in these action-packed retellings from Anthony Horowitz

L E G E N D S
TRICKS AND TRANSFORMATIONS

You might consider yourself a master
of **pranks** and **practical jokes**.
But throughout time there are those who
truly deserve the name **trickster** –
read their stories and you will soon
discover you have much to learn . . .

**Rediscover classic myths and legends in these
action-packed retellings from Anthony Horowitz**